PALATINE PUBLIC LIBRARY
3 1265 01603 9507

W9-BRE-412

BRAM

SKSSSHHH
BRMB

WHD

KCHUNK

BRRRRMMMM

THEY'RE STILL BEHIND US!
SO THAT'S A NO FOR PLAN B.

MANAGEMENT IS NOW ACCEPTING SUGGESTIONS FOR PLAN C!

THUNK

VRMMMMMB

REN-
RNNNNAH

ANYTIME YOU FEEL LIKE --
I'M THINKING!

WELL, THINK FASTER, CLEM. WE'RE CLOSE!
I KNOW, I KNOW!
100
20
80
140
60
mph
160
CLANG!
WE'RE SO CLOSE.

BLUP
BLUP
BLUP

SHARP LEFT!

BLOUB
BLOUB
ROGER THAT!

CLINK!
BOOSH!
CRUNCH
GAH!
UH!
HEE
HEE.

I'M LOSING CONTROL, DIG!
DO SOMETHING!
LIKE WHAT?!
ANYTHING!

HNNNN --
WRENCH

HUH?

SEE HOW YOU LIKE THAT!

CLANG!
CLONG

YEP, THAT'LL DO IT!

OBSTACLE STRAIGHT AHEAD!
HUH?
IS THAT--?

THUNT!
SKSHH
CLEM!

CLEM HETHE

AND THE IRONW

RINGTON

DOD RACE

BY JEN BREACH & DOUGLAS HOLGATE

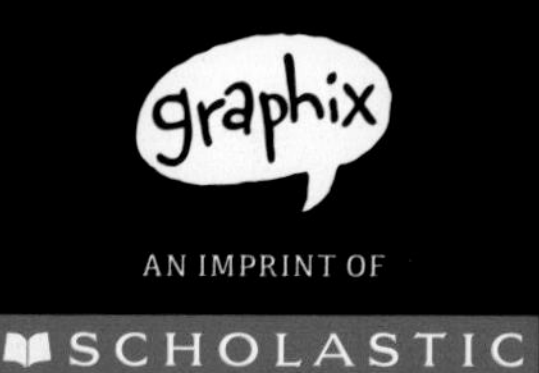

AN IMPRINT OF
SCHOLASTIC

LAST WEEK
PROFESSOR E. R. J. PERTON
ARCHAEOLOGIST

PROFESSOR E. R. J. PERTON
ARCHAEOLOGIST

KNOCK
KNOCK
KNOCK

COMING!
JUST A MO--
OOF!
CRASH!

PROFESSOR E. R. J. PE
ARCHAEOLOGIST.
YES?
HELLO, PROFESSOR.

CLEMENTINE HETHERINGTON!

THANK GOODNESS YOU'RE SAFE!

COME IN, COME IN.
SORRY FOR THE MESS, I JUST KNOCKED OVER A STACK OF PAPERS.
MUST'VE BEEN SOME STACK.

PLEASE, SIT DOWN, SIT DOWN.

THE POLICE ARE LOOKING FOR YOU, CLEM.

THE ORPHANAGE, TOO!

I KNOW.

CLEM, ARE YOU ALL RIGHT?
WHERE ARE YOU STAYING?
ARE YOU HUNGRY?
WHERE'S DIGORY?

I'M FINE, PROFESSOR, REALLY.
DIG IS LOOKING AFTER ME.
YES, GOOD, GOOD.
DIGORY WILL ALWAYS KEEP YOU SAFE.

PROFESSOR, WE NEED YOUR HELP.
ANYTHING, CLEM.
WE NEED TO GET BACK INTO THE FIELD.
WE NEED YOU TO TAKE US ON AN EXCAVATION.

OF COURSE.
REALLY?

YES!
THE CEREMONIAL ARMOR AND WEAPONRY YOU EXCAVATED ON THE ELECOURT DIG REVOLUTIONIZED THE WAY WE THINK ABOUT SUMA. AND YOU WERE ONLY NINE THEN!
THAT'S RIGHT.

GOODNESS! JUST IMAGINE HOW EXTRAORDINARY YOU'LL BE AFTER COLLEGE! I'D LOVE TO HAVE YOU ON THE TEAM THEN.
AFTER COLLEGE?
YES, FINISH SCHOOL, GET INSTITUTE ACCREDITATION -- I'LL WRITE YOU A VERY SUPPORTIVE LETTER -- THEN COME SEE ME.

I MEANT NOW. TAKE US ON YOUR NEXT DIG.
CLEM, YOU'RE FOURTEEN YEARS OLD! YOU'RE NOT AN ARCHAEOLOGIST, YOU'RE A CHILD!

YOU'RE WRONG ABOUT THAT.
ON BOTH COUNTS.

MOM AND DAD RAISED ME AND DIG ON ARCHAEOLOGICAL SITES AROUND THE WORLD!
UNEARTHING THE WORLD'S TREASURES. UNDERSTANDING PEOPLE THROUGH THE THINGS THEY LEFT BEHIND.

NOTHING ELSE MATTERS TO ME.
YES, YES, IT'S ALL VERY IMPORTANT, EXCITING WORK.
IT'S SO DIFFICULT NOT KNOWING WHAT HAPPENED TO YOUR PARENTS...

I'M NOT INDIFFERENT TO THAT. BUT, CLEM, WITH YOUR MOM GONE, THERE'S NO ONE TO VOUCH FOR YOU.
I'M VOUCHING FOR ME!

LET ME CALL THE ORPHANAGE SO THEY CAN COME COLLECT YOU.
I'LL VISIT YOU NEXT WEEK AND BRING THE PLANS FOR THE TRAVELING EXHIBIT OF YOUR MOTHER'S MUSHA FINDS.

IT WAS A MISTAKE TO COME HERE.
CLEM, WAIT!

SLAM!

POLICE.
MISSING PERSONS, PLEASE.

WE CAN GO NOW, DIG.

HOW'D IT GO WITH PROFESSOR PERTON?
HE SAID WE SHOULD GO BACK TO THE ORPHANAGE. GO BACK TO SCHOOL, COME SEE HIM IN NINE YEARS.

OH, CLEM, I'M SORRY.
IT'S BEEN THREE MONTHS, DIG.
PERTON WAS OUR LAST HOPE.
I HAVE NO IDEA OF WHAT WE'RE GOING TO DO NOW.

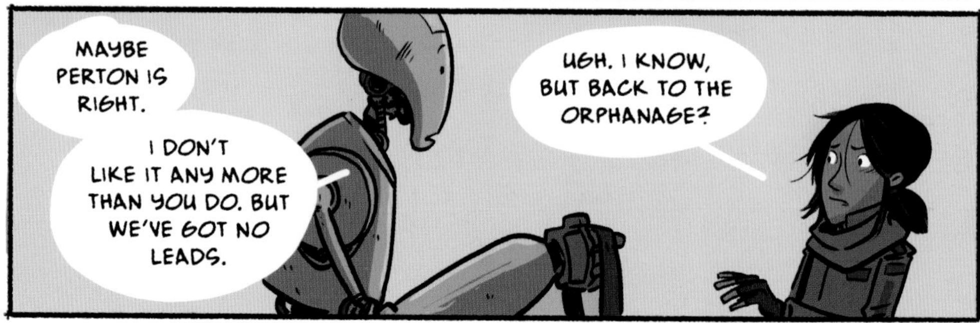
MAYBE PERTON IS RIGHT.
I DON'T LIKE IT ANY MORE THAN YOU DO. BUT WE'VE GOT NO LEADS.
UGH. I KNOW, BUT BACK TO THE ORPHANAGE?

MOM BECAME AN ARCHAEOLOGIST BY GOING THROUGH THE SYSTEM.
MAYBE THAT'S THE WAY WE SHOULD DO IT, TOO.
IT SOUNDS EXHAUSTING.

NOTHING ELSE IS WORKING OUT. WE'LL HAVE TO GO BACK.
BUT -- NOT JUST YET? GIVE IT A COUPLE MORE DAYS.
ALL RIGHT. MAYBE WE'LL THINK OF SOMETHING.

OPEN

IN THE MEANTIME, LET ME BUY YOU A DONUT TO CHEER YOU UP.
A DOLLAR IS WAY TOO EXPENSIVE.
WE CAN'T AFFORD THAT.
DONUTS $1

OH. YOU'RE RIGHT, WE CAN'T.

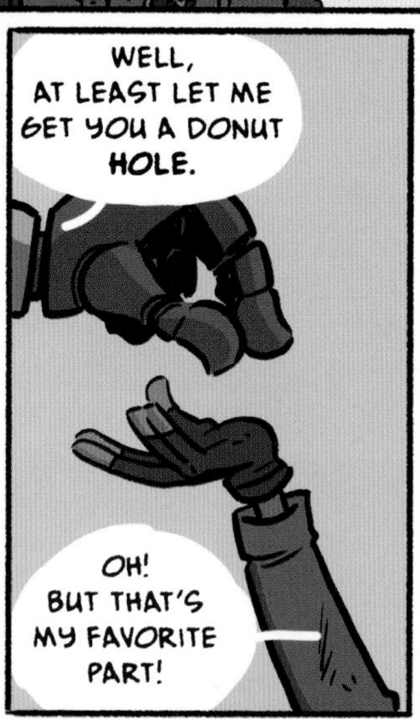
WELL, AT LEAST LET ME GET YOU A DONUT HOLE.
OH! BUT THAT'S MY FAVORITE PART!

ALL AT ONCE? GREEDY!
SMACK
SMACK
SMACK
I CAN'T HELP MYSELF! SO DELICIOUS!

DON'T WORRY, I'LL GET US SOME MORE MONEY IN THE MORNING. AND THEN YOU CAN HAVE TWO DONUT HOLES.
SUCH EXTRAVAGANCE!

ARE YOU EVER GOING TO TELL ME WHERE YOU GET THE MONEY FROM?

PROBABLY NOT, NO.

JUST TELL ME IT'S NOTHING DANGEROUS.
IT'S NOT, I PROMISE.

THE PRESCHOOLERS AND LITTLE OLD LADIES I STEAL FROM HARDLY EVER FIGHT BACK.

WHAT WOULD I DO WITHOUT YOU, DIGORY?
SAME THING I'D DO WITHOUT YOU. FALL APART?
EXCUSE ME, SIR?

HAVE YOU SEEN THIS GIRL?
SHE'S MISSING BUT MIGHT BE IN THE AREA.
UH-OH.
NAH, I HAVEN'T SEEN HER.
OKAY. THANKS FOR YOUR TIME.
SURE.

TINK

K-TINK

GOAL!
TUNG!
T-TINK
TINK

HOME
SWEET HOME.

?!

THOSE STREET HOODS BROKE OUR LAST WINDOW!

CALM DOWN, DIG.
THEY THINK THE BUILDING'S ABANDONED. THAT'S THE POINT, REMEMBER?
I KNOW, I KNOW.
BUT STILL.
TO MAKE IT LOOK LIKE NO ONE LIVES HERE.

IT'S GOING TO RAIN TONIGHT. YOU SHOULD SLEEP IN THE DRY CORNER.
THE RAIN IS EXACTLY WHY YOU NEED THE DRY CORNER.

YOU KNOW
I CAN'T FIX YOU IF
YOU SHORT OUT. KEEPING
YOU GOING IS WORTH A
SOGGY NIGHT'S
SLEEP.
ALL
RIGHT.

BZZT

BZZT

BZZT

PLINK

THAT'S THE STUFF. I'M BEAT, CLEM.
I'M GOING TO CLOSE MY EYES.
SLUMP

SURE, DIG. GOOD NIGHT.
SCRAPE

TOSS

KA-BOOM!

PLINK
PLINK
PLINK

SIGH.

TOSS

BA-
BOOM!

WHO ARE YOU?!

WHAT IS IT? WHAT -- GUH!

WHAT'S HAPPENING?!

KILBURN?!
HI, CLEM. LONG TIME NO SEE.

KILBURN?!
HELLO, DIG.

DARTH VADER HIMSELF. HOW IS THE DARK SIDE OF ARCHAEOLOGY?
OH, IT'S FINE. LUCRATIVE LIKE YOU WOULDN'T BELIEVE.

HOW DID YOU FIND US?
IT WASN'T EASY, THAT'S FOR SURE.

I'M MORE INTERESTED IN WHY YOU FOUND US.

THE SHORT VERSION IS THAT I NEED YOUR HELP.
THAT'S THE LONG VERSION AND IT'S, WELL, LONGER.
NEED OUR HELP WITH WHAT?
GO ON.

YOU KNOW I'VE BEEN AN ARCHAEOLOGIST IN THE PRIVATE MARKET SINCE DR. HETHERINGTON AND YOUR DAD DIED.
YOU MEAN THE **BLACK** MARKET, KILBURN, LET'S NOT GET FANCY.

I'M UNDERTAKING A VERY... **SPECIFIC** EXPEDITION. I NEED AN UNBEATABLE FIELD TEAM.

AND I WANT YOU.
IT WASN'T THAT MUCH LONGER THAN THE SHORT VERSION.

WAIT. YOU'RE OFFERING US A JOB?
YES.
ON A DIG?
EXACTLY.

I DON'T WORK FOR TRAITORS, KILBURN, OR LIARS. SO THAT'S YOU OUT ON TWO COUNTS, ISN'T IT?

DON'T BE AN IDIOT. IT'LL PAY WELL.
DON'T TALK TO HER LIKE THAT.

BUT THIS IS EXACTLY WHAT WE WANT, RIGHT?
IT IS, BUT -- WHY DOES IT HAVE TO BE KILBURN?

UNLESS YOU'VE GIVEN UP ARCHAEOLOGY ALTOGETHER FOR THIS SWANKY NEW LIFE.

WHICH WOULD BE A SHAME.

NOTHING'S BEEN LIKE IT SHOULD BE SINCE YOUR PARENTS DIED.
I MISS YOU GUYS.

WE WERE A GREAT TEAM ON DR. HETHERINGTON'S DIGS, WEREN'T WE?
YES.
WE COULD BE AGAIN.

BUT WE'D HAVE TO CLEAN YOU UP FIRST. YOU LOOK TERRIBLE.
I HAVE A STATE-OF-THE-ART MECH LAB. THEY'D HAVE YOU UPGRADED AND POLISHED IN NO TIME.

IN FACT, THEY COULD PROBABLY --
DON'T TOUCH HIM.

OKAY, OKAY. DON'T TALK TO YOU LIKE THAT, DON'T TOUCH HIM. LOTS OF GROUND RULES AROUND HERE.

LOOK. THERE ARE A LOT LESS HIGH FIVES, GROUP HUGS, AND SAYING YES GOING ON HERE THAN I HAD ANTICIPATED.
WHAT GIVES?

I DON'T TRUST YOU.

WHEN OUR PARENTS DIED, WE NEEDED YOU.
AT THE FUNERAL, YOU SAID...

I WILL ALWAYS BE HERE FOR YOU. WE'RE IN THIS TOGETHER NOW.

AND THEN YOU DISAPPEARED!
FOR THREE YEARS!

WHEN THEY PUT US IN THE ORPHANAGE YOU NEVER EVEN VISITED US.
I COULDN'T. IT WAS -- YOU IN THAT PLACE? IT WAS TOO MUCH.

WE WOULDN'T HAVE BEEN THERE AT ALL IF YOU HAD ADOPTED US.
WE WOULD HAVE FIGURED IT OUT **TOGETHER.** AFTER OUR PARENTS DIED, YOU WERE THE ONLY FAMILY WE HAD LEFT.

BUT YOU ABANDONED US. RIGHT WHEN WE NEEDED YOU MOST.
HE'LL COME TOMORROW, CLEM. I KNOW HE'LL COME FOR US TOMORROW.

I KNOW. I'M SORRY.

LET ME MAKE IT RIGHT.
COME ON THIS DIG WITH ME.

NO. WE'LL GET ON ANOTHER DIG.

YOU SURE ABOUT THAT? I KNOW YOU SAW PERTON TODAY AND HE'S NOT GOING TO HELP YOU. I THINK YOU'RE OUT OF OPTIONS.
I JUST -- I JUST NEED TO FIGURE IT OUT.

CALL ME IF YOU CHANGE YOUR MIND. AND PLEASE DON'T RELOCATE.
IT WAS HARD ENOUGH TO FIND YOU THIS TIME.

ALISTAIR KILBURN
Private Archaeologist
xpeditions - Consultations - Acquisitions

THE NEXT MORNING

SIGH.

GONE TO ROB LITTLE OLD LADIES!! BACK SOON D.

GONE
TO ROB
LITTLE OLD
LADIES!! BACK
SOON,

TAKE IT ALL. THIS DUDE GIVES GARBAGE SPARK, ANYWAY.
NO, PLEASE.
YEAH! AND IF WE TAKE IT ALL, WE WON'T HAVE TO PAY HIM FOR IT!
ALMOST THERE...

DIGORY?

DIGORY!

SOMEONE'S COMING! HURRY UP!

GOT IT!

GOT YOU!

OOF!
CLANG!

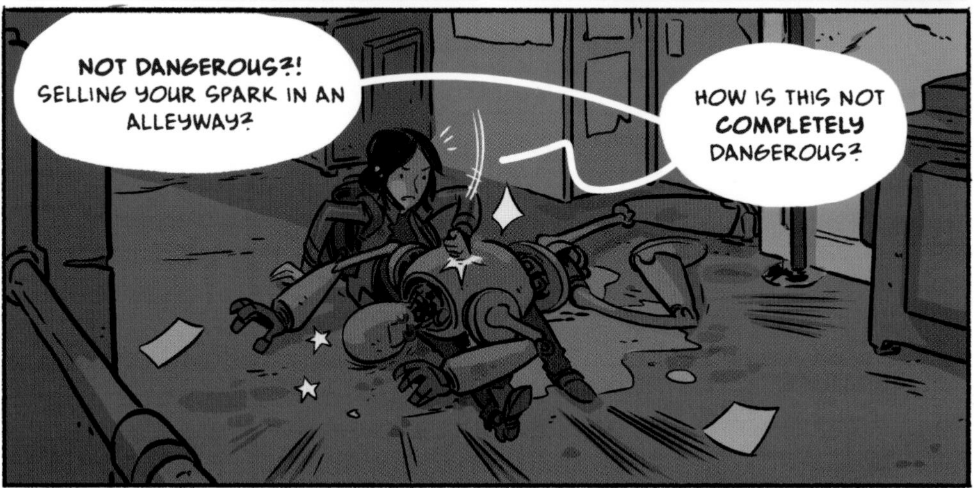
NOT DANGEROUS?! SELLING YOUR SPARK IN AN ALLEYWAY?
HOW IS THIS NOT COMPLETELY DANGEROUS?

DIG?
DIGORY!

OH NO, OH NO, OH NO.

NO.

I DON'T -- HELP!
SOMEBODY HELP!

I DON'T KNOW HOW TO FIX YOU.

I DON'T KNOW HOW TO FIX YOU!
BANG!

WAIT --

WAIT
A MINUTE.

UGH.

COME
ON.

AGH, NO!
UGH. GET UP, CLEMENTINE.
GET.
UP!

GENTLY.
GENTLY.

KILBURN.
BAM!
THE STATE-OF-THE-ART MECH LAB.

WHAT--?!
WHUMP!

FIX HIM.

YOU FIX HIM AND I'LL COME ON YOUR STUPID DIG.

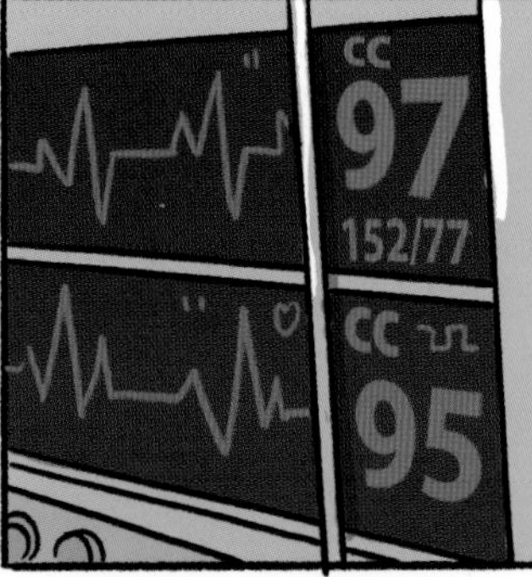
CC
97
152/77
CC
95

COMMENCING PROCEDURE.
MAKING PRIMARY INCISION.

THIS'LL BE A TOUGH ONE, FOLKS, BUT HE'S GOTTA PULL THROUGH.
DON'T WORRY, CLEM, THESE GUYS ARE THE BEST.

I DON'T KNOW WHAT I'D DO IF -- I JUST DON'T KNOW WHAT --

HE JUST BETTER NOT DIE IS ALL.

I'M SORRY, CLEM, BUT I REALLY HAVE SOME WORK I NEED TO GET BACK --
SO GO.

Z Z Z Z

CLEM...
CLEM.
WH--?

WAKE UP, CHUCKLEHEAD.
DIG?

DIG!
HIYA, CLEM.

ARE YOU OKAY? HOW DO YOU FEEL?
I'M FINE, CLEM, GOOD AS NEW.

TIME IS SHORT. MEET ME AT THE CAR.
THE CAR?

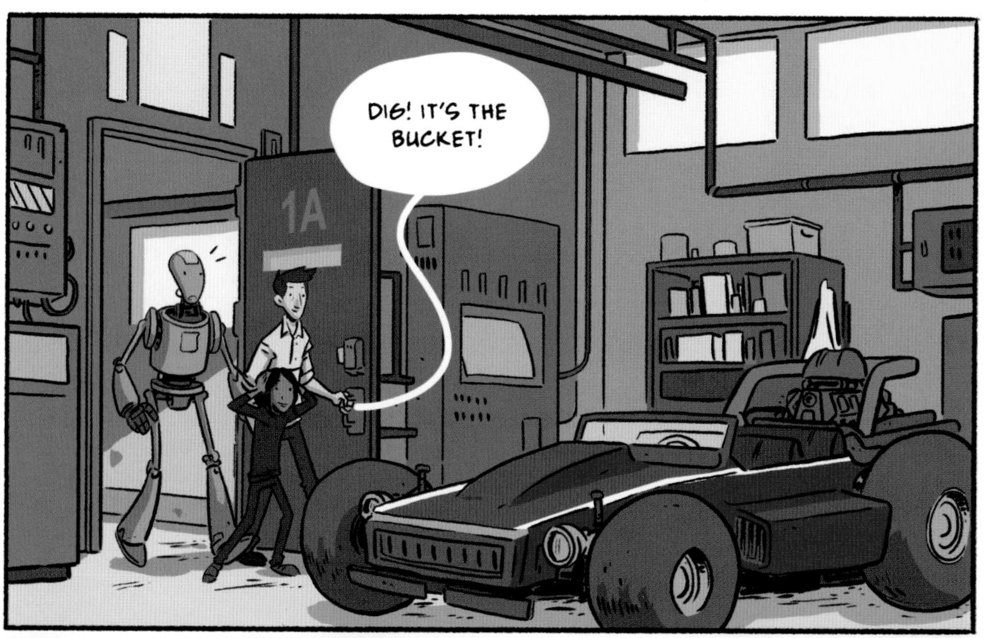
DIG! IT'S THE BUCKET!

BUT HOW? THE ORPHANAGE LOCKED HER UP.

PFFT. I WOULDN'T CALL THAT **LOCKED** UP.
YOU STOLE HER?
TECHNICALLY.

AND SHE'S SO SHINY!
I HAD THE MECH GUYS CLEAN HER UP. THEY TRIED TO TUNE HER, TOO, BUT THEY COULDN'T MAKE HEADS OR TAILS OF THE ENGINE.

DAD BUILT THIS WHOLE MACHINE FROM SCRATCH, THE ENGINE AND EVERYTHING. HE BUILT IT JUST FOR ME.

THEN YOU'D BETTER DRIVE. WE'RE ALREADY LATE.

LATE FOR WHAT, EXACTLY?

THE STARTING LINE.
SINCE WHEN DO ARCHAEOLOGICAL DIGS HAVE STARTING LINES?

IT'S CALLED **THE IRONWOOD RACE**. IT'S A MULTIDAY RALLY RACE TO ARCHAEOLOGICAL SITES FOR COMPETITIVE DIGGING.

THAT SOUNDS **AWESOME.**

I THOUGHT IT MIGHT APPEAL.

THIS SAYS THE IRONWOOD RACE IS PART OF A LARGER COMPETITION OF SOME KIND. WHAT'S THAT?
I DON'T KNOW.

WELL, THAT'S USEFUL.

NOBODY KNOWS. THE COMPETITION HAS BEEN GOING FOR HUNDREDS OF YEARS. NO ONE KNOWS HOW IT STARTED, AND NO ONE KNOWS WHEN IT'LL END.
HUH.

SO, LOOKS LIKE WE'LL BE DIGGING FOR A GOLD PUCOON NECK RING, A STATUETTE OF A ZYGLIAN CREATOR GOD, A STASH OF TWO DOZEN AMASTROAN COINS, AND A SIXTEENTH-CENTURY CHOETIAN DAGGER.
Leg 1

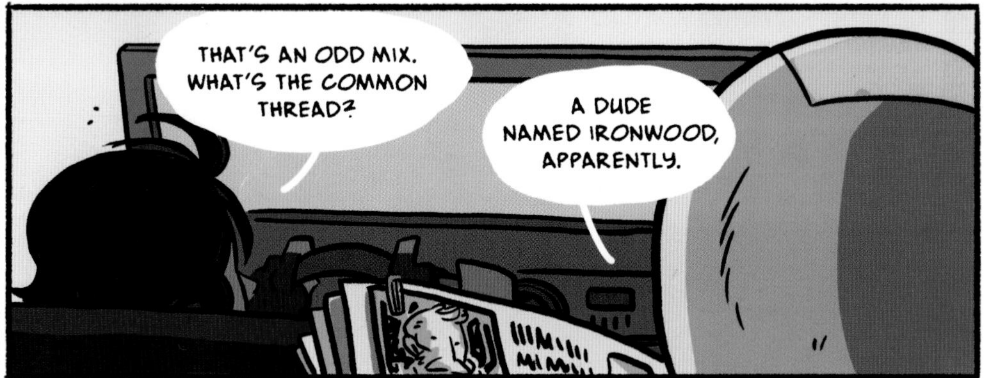

THAT'S AN ODD MIX. WHAT'S THE COMMON THREAD?
A DUDE NAMED IRONWOOD, APPARENTLY.

WHAT, LIKE IRONWOOD THE TOMB RAIDER?
WHO?

LET'S SEE. BRECHT IRONWOOD, BORN IN LONDON IN 1873. DISAPPEARED AND PRESUMED DEAD IN 1956.

INSTEAD OF ACQUIRING ARTIFACTS FOR MUSEUM COLLECTIONS, HE STARTED SELLING THEM ON THE BLACK MARKET.
OH, SO HE'S A SCUMBAG.
YES AND NO. AFTER A DECADE OF STEALING ARTIFACTS, HE HAD AN EPIPHANY AND TRIED TO MAKE IT RIGHT.

HE SPENT HIS ENTIRE FORTUNE TRYING TO BUY BACK THE ARTIFACTS HE SOLD ON THE BLACK MARKET -- GET THIS --
SO HE COULD PUT THEM BACK.
SERIOUSLY?

IT'S INCREDIBLE, RIGHT? SO...NOBLE.

PFFT. NOBLE? IT WAS **MADNESS**. THERE WAS NOTHING TO BE GAINED FROM IT.
GAIN ISN'T EVERYTHING, KILBURN. HE WAS DOING WHAT HE THOUGHT WAS RIGHT.

TOO BAD HE NEVER PULLED IT OFF.

HE DID. ONCE.
IS THAT WHAT EXPLAINOPEDIA TOLD YOU?

TOWARD THE END, HE'D RUN OUT OF MONEY AND CRED. DESPERATE, HE STOLE FOUR ARTIFACTS FROM A PRIVATE COLLECTOR HE'D BEEN SUPPLYING --
A GUY IN A KIND OF MAFIA.

SOUNDS LIKE OUR BOY HAD SOME SUCCESS AFTER ALL. WHAT HAPPENED THEN?

HE BURIED THEM IN THE DESERT NOT FAR FROM HERE BEFORE THE GANGSTER CAUGHT UP WITH HIM...
AND THAT WAS THE END OF THAT.

WHICH BRINGS US BACK TO THE IRONWOOD RACE --
A RACE TO FIND THE FOUR MISSING IRONWOOD ARTIFACTS.

WOW, MYTH CHASING. THAT'S NOT SOMETHING I THOUGHT I'D DO BEFORE, WELL, EVER.

WHAT HAPPENS TO THE ARTIFACTS ONCE THEY'RE EXCAVATED AGAIN?
THEY BECOME THE RACE PRIZES. WHEN YOU WIN, YOU GET TO KEEP THEM.
OR, MORE LIKELY, SELL THEM ON THE PRIVATE MARKET AND GET VERY, VERY RICH!

OR DONATE THEM TO PERTON AND THE LEWISHON MUSEUM.

THIS INSTRUCTION PACKET DOESN'T SAY MUCH ABOUT THE RACE RULES.

PROBABLY BECAUSE THERE AREN'T ANY.

WHAT?!

THERE ARE NO RULES, BUT THERE'S A CODE. THE TEAM THAT RACES THE FASTEST, DIGS THE MOST ARTIFACTS, AND CROSSES THE FINISH LINE WINS. WINNER TAKES ALL.
BUT APART FROM THAT, BETWEEN STARTING GUN AND FINISH LINE? ANYTHING GOES.

SO THIS IS A RACE WHERE NOTHING IS ILLEGAL?
CLEM, THE WHOLE RACE IS ILLEGAL.

SO IS UNDERAGE DRIVING, I GUESS.

BRUM
BRUM
BRUM
BRUM
WE'RE HERE.

TEAM HETHERINGTON SIGNING IN.
ALISTAIR KILBURN, THEIR MANAGER.
AND YOU ARE?

HOLY.
COW.

ALRIGHTY. YOUR ENTRANCE FEE IS FULLY PAID, SO I JUST NEED YOU TO SIGN HERE.

AND HERE.
WOULD YOU JUST LOOK AT THESE GUYS, CLEM?

INITIAL HERE.
I DON'T EVEN KNOW WHAT HALF THIS STUFF IS.

AND ONE LAST SIGNATURE HERE.
I'M NOT SURE WHAT I WAS EXPECTING. BUT IT WASN'T THIS.
AND YOU'RE ALL SET.

WE NEED TO WIN THIS THING, DIG. THE LOST IRONWOOD TREASURES? IF WE BRING THEM TO THE LEWISHON MUSEUM, WE'LL BE INDUSTRY HEROES AND PROFESSOR PERTON WILL **HAVE** TO TAKE US SERIOUSLY.
I'M ON BOARD. BUT WIN? HOW?

DON'T WORRY. THE FIELD LOOKS MORE COMPETITIVE THAN IT REALLY IS. MOST OF THESE JOKERS WON'T EVEN FINISH THE FIRST DAY.

THE ONLY TEAMS YOU NEED TO WORRY ABOUT ARE...

TEAM DRAY. THEY'RE REALLY SMART.

AND TEAM CROCODILLO. THEY'RE REALLY MEAN.

AND YOU ONLY NEED THREE THINGS TO WIN THIS RACE.
WHAT ARE THEY?

A TROWEL...
A CAR...

THAT'S ONLY TWO THINGS.

AND A CRAP-TON OF LUCK.

COME ON, RACE STARTS AT SUNRISE AND WE NEED TO BRIEF TOMORROW'S DIG.

TOMORROW'S ARTIFACT IS THE DAGGER, ALSO KNOWN AS THE STAR OF THE EAST. CLEARLY, YOU SHOULD DIG FOR IT HERE -- TO THE EAST.

BEST STRATEGY IS TO DRIVE HARD, GET IN FRONT EARLY, AND BUILD A GOOD LEAD TO GIVE YOU MORE TIME AT THE DIG SITE.

EXCEPT HEADING EAST WOULD MEAN DIGGING IN THE WRONG SPOT.

I'M SORRY?
YORKE CITES CONSIDERABLE EVIDENCE IN HIS SCHOLARLY WORK ON THE CHOETIAN THAT **STAR** IS A MISTRANSLATION. IT SHOULD BE **SOUTH**.
SOUTH OF THE EAST?

EXACTLY. WE SHOULD BE DIGGING IN THE SOUTHEAST.
WELL, THAT'S...BRILLIANT, CLEM.

IT'S ONLY BRILLIANT IF YOU'RE RIGHT.
OF COURSE I'M RIGHT.
HM.

MOVING ON TO WEAPONS.
WHOA! WHAT IS **THAT**?!

AN RG-90 MACKENZIE LOCK-BARREL PROJECTILE LAUNCHER. IT'S AN OLDER MODEL, WHICH MIGHT BE BETTER BECAUSE YOU WON'T NEED TO AIM SO PRECISELY.
AIM AT WHAT, EXACTLY?
THE OTHER CARS, OF COURSE.

NO. ABSOLUTELY NOT.
EVERYONE OUT THERE WILL HAVE HARDWARE LIKE THIS. YOU'LL NEED TO BE ABLE TO PROTECT YOURSELF.

THEN WE'LL FIGURE SOMETHING ELSE OUT. PUT IT AWAY.

YOU REMIND ME SO MUCH OF YOUR MOTHER, CLEM.

WE SHOULD REST. IT'S BEEN A BIG DAY.

AND TOMORROW WILL BE BIGGER.

IRONWOOD RACE: DAY 1
FSST
FSST
FSSST

CHUNG
CHUNG
CHUNG
BZZZT
BZZT
GRRN
GRRRN!

DIGORY, DID YOU UPLOAD THOSE NEW MAPS?
RIGHT HERE, KILBURN.
GOOD.

START SLOW AND HANG BACK SO YOU CAN SWING SOUTHEAST WITHOUT GETTING TOO MUCH ATTENTION.

THE START CAN BE A LITTLE...CHAOTIC. BE CAREFUL.
JUST LIKE WE TALKED ABOUT.

ARE YOU READY FOR THIS, CLEM?
I'VE GOT A TROWEL AND A CAR. LET'S FIND OUT ABOUT THAT LUCK.
ATTAGIRL.

ARCHAEOLOGISTS! START. YOUR. ENGINES!

BRAM! BRAM! BRA
BRAM! BRA
BNNNN!
RNGG!
GET SET!

RNNN!

GREE

RNNG!
RNNG!

GO!

SKSSHH

THUNK

BAM!

HEY!
A LITTLE CHAOTIC?!

GRNNN
WHAT--?

SKRRRT

THEY'RE GOING TO CUT US OFF!

SKSHHH!

BAM!

WE'RE OUT OF THE RACE BECAUSE OF YOU!
YOU TRY DRIVING WITH A SHREDDED TIRE!

THAT -- THAT COULD HAVE BEEN US!

QUICK, DIG, I NEED YOUR EYES ON THE FIELD!
TELL ME WHAT YOU SEE!

I'VE GOT THREE ON THE LEFT, FOUR ON THE RIGHT, AND TWO BEHIND. YOU?

I'VE GOT...LOTS! I'VE GOT LOTS!

I DON'T THINK ANY OF THEM ARE GUNNING FOR US, THOUGH.
OKAY, GOOD. LET'S NOT GET IN THEIR WAY.
ROGER THAT.

I THINK THEY'RE GUNNING FOR TEAM DRAY.
BAAAAWHN

BOOSH!
GNNN
THUD

WOW! SHE CAN REALLY DRIVE.

BAM!

WHOA!
SKSHHHH!

GRRNNNN!

KRAK!

BOMP!

BOOM!

BAM!

CLEM! LOOK OUT!

NICE.
SKSSSH!
THANKS.

YEP, DAD KNEW WHAT HE WAS DOING WHEN HE BUILT THE BUCKET.
PAT PAT

BEEP
BEEP
BEEP

OR NOT?

BETTER EASE DOWN, CLEM. SHE CAN'T RUN AT THIS PACE FOR LONG.
I KNOW.

THERE'S A GAP YOU CAN DROP BACK INTO. YOUR SEVEN O'CLOCK.

ROGER THAT.

GRNNNN

THAT MIGHT BE SOMETHING OVER THERE. BEAR SLIGHTLY RIGHT.
I SEE IT.

LOOK AT THE WAY THE EARTH IS SLIGHTLY SUNKEN HERE.

THIS IS IT.
WELL, IT'S SOMETHING. LET'S SEE IF IT'S THE STAR OF THE EAST.

NOT ANOTHER CAR IN SIGHT.

SINCE IRONWOOD REBURIED THE STAR THERE PROBABLY WON'T BE SOIL STRATA, BUT I'LL TAKE THE TOPSOIL SAMPLE ANYWAY.
THERE PROBABLY WON'T BE ANY OTHER MATERIAL OF INTEREST AT ALL.
THE STAR WILL BE ENOUGH.
RIGHT?

DIGORY.

THIS --

I KNOW.
NOW, DIG.

SCRAPE

BRRNNN

SCREEECH!

HUH?
WHAT --
WHAT'S GOING ON?
QUIT SHOVING!

LEG WINNER: TEAM HETHERINGTON!

DID HE SAY HETHERINGTON?

NICE WORK, HETHERINGTON.

OH! UH, THANKS, MS. DRAY!

I'LL HAVE TO KEEP MY EYE ON YOU.

WOW.

CLEM, YOU'RE A NATURAL!

YOU WERE AMAZING. I'M SO PROUD.
YOUR PARENTS WOULD BE, TOO.

WHERE'S DIG?
HE'S RESEARCHING WHAT WE'RE UP AGAINST.

WE WERE CAUGHT BY SURPRISE OUT THERE TODAY. I DON'T WANT IT TO HAPPEN AGAIN.

CONGRATULATIONS, MS. HETHERINGTON. I'LL TAKE THE FIND FOR THE RACE PRIZE NOW.

THANK YOU. GOOD LUCK TOMORROW.
IT'S BEAUTIFUL. THIS WILL GET A GREAT PRICE.

WE'RE NOT SELLING IT. IF WE WIN, THE ARTIFACTS GO TO PERTON AND THE MUSEUM. THOSE ARE MY TERMS.

THE DEAL WAS I FIX DIGORY AND YOU JOIN THE DIG. THAT'S WHAT I AGREED TO.
AND I'VE DONE MY PART.

YOU NEED US, KILBURN. I KNOW THIS DIG IS NOT ENTIRELY ABOVE-BOARD FOR YOU.
FIRST, WHY AREN'T WE TAPPING YOUR MASSIVELY WELL-RESOURCED LAB FOR A SUPPORT TEAM?

SECOND, YOU'RE A BRILLIANT **ARCHAEOLOGIST**. IF YOU COULD, YOU'D DO THIS YOURSELF.
AND THIRD, YOU'RE **GREEDY**. YOU WOULDN'T SPLIT WINNINGS IF YOU HAD A CHOICE.

IT'S TRUE.
I CAN'T RUN THE RACE MYSELF. I'M LAYING LOW BECAUSE I'M IN DEBT... A **LOT** OF IT...
AND THE RACE WINNINGS ARE MY BEST SHOT AT GETTING CLEAR.

YES, I NEED YOU.
BUT NEVER FORGET THAT YOU WOULDN'T EVEN BE HERE IF IT WASN'T FOR ME.

IT'S BAD.
THESE CARS ARE ARMED TO THE HILT. TIRE SHREDDERS, GRAPPLING HOOKS, FLAMETHROWERS, AND I DON'T EVEN KNOW WHAT ELSE.

AND IT GETS WORSE. THEY'VE REALIZED WE'RE THE KIDS OF THE GREAT DR. HETHERINGTON.
OH.

WE'RE GOING TO GET A LOT OF ATTENTION ON THE TRACK TOMORROW. IT COULD GET REALLY MESSY.

AHEM.

ALL RIGHT. BUT YOU'LL NEED TO TEACH ME HOW TO USE IT.

IRONWOOD RACE: DAY 2

RACE LEG
STAR OF THE EAST
STATUETTE OF FALJEN
PUCOON NECK RING
AMASTROAN
TEAM HETHERINGTON

HOW COME THEY'RE STILL RACING? I SAW THEM CRASH OUT YESTERDAY.

A CAR IS CONSIDERED DISQUALIFIED ONLY IF IT CAN'T BE REPAIRED IN TIME FOR THE STARTING GUN THE NEXT DAY.

I'D BE HAPPIER IF WE HAD A SUPPORT CREW, A MECHANIC. SOMEONE WHO COULD GET US RUNNING AGAIN IF THE BUCKET BREAKS DOWN.

DO YOU KNOW YOUR WAY AROUND AN ENGINE?
?!

NOT AT ALL.
ALL I KNOW IS THAT IT'S THE BIT THAT GETS REALLY LOUD WHEN I PRESS THE GAS.

NONE OF THE MECHS AT MY, AS YOU SAY, **MASSIVELY WELL-RESOURCED LAB** COULD FIGURE HER OUT, SO I DON'T KNOW WHAT GOOD THEY'D BE.

JUST...DON'T BREAK DOWN.

THE STATUETTE OF FALJEN, ZYGLIAN CREATOR GOD. THIRD INTERMEDIATE PERIOD, 900 BC.
YEAH.

IT'S MAGNIFICENT. CAN YOU IMAGINE WHAT IT WOULD BE LIKE TO HOLD IT?

JUST WAIT UNTIL THE END OF THE DAY. THEN YOU'LL BE ABLE TO IMAGINE IT REALLY WELL.

ARCHAEOLOGISTS! START. YOUR. ENGINES!
GOOD LUCK, YOU GUYS.
DON'T NEED IT, KILBURN.

ACTUALLY, WE PROBABLY DO.
GET SET!

GO!

BAM

WHERE DID HE COME FROM?!

UH!
WHAM!

WE'RE PINNED!

OKAY, THEN.

THAT'S IT!

NO!

NICE TRY, LITTLE GIRL.

CLEM, THAT ROCK UP AHEAD, THEY'RE --
I SEE IT.

FASTER, CLEM. GO FASTER!
NO. WAIT.
UH... PLEASE?

NOT FASTER.

WHUD

SKSHHHH!

BABOOM!

OH MY
GOSH.

BRM
BRM
BRM

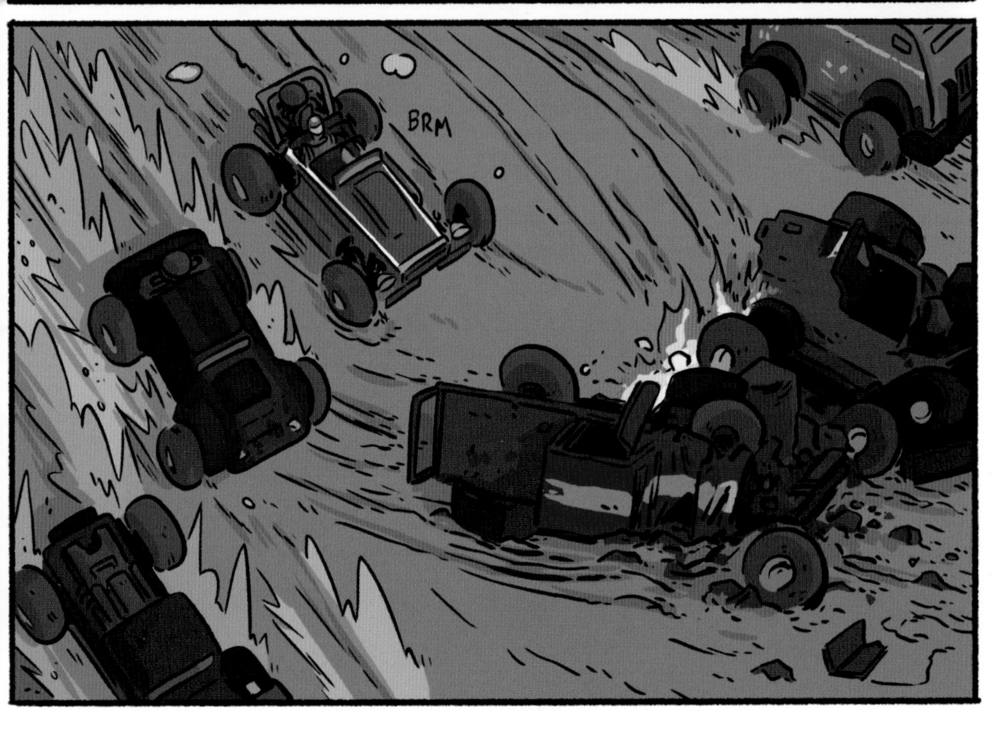
BRM

I'VE GOT TWO ON MY SIDE, ONE ON YOURS, AND FOUR DIRECTLY BEHIND. WE'VE GOT TO MOVE.

KCHUNK

BRRMMN
SKSHHH
ROGER THAT!

BAAAHNNN!

WHUMP

SSKSHHH

LET'S SEE HOW THIS GOES.

CLICK
ZMMMM

BOOSH
DARN!

GET IT TOGETHER, DIGORY.
SHUNT!

FUD

THIS TIME.

BOOSH

YES!
DONK!

CRACK
POK!

WHOOOOA!

PUNCH IT, CLEM!
PUNCHING IT!

GNNNNNH

GRNNNNN!

BOM!

BOM!

SPLOT

CRACK

RELOADING

I'VE GOT NOTHING UNTIL IT RELOADS!

ARCHAEOLOGISTS WITH A MACE AND A BAD ATTITUDE CLOSING IN AT EIGHT O'CLOCK.

OKAY, DIG, I GOT THIS.

THUD

CHUNG
CHUNG
CHUNG
CHUNG

BOOM

ENOUGH ALREADY.

SHUNK!

BRNNN!

BONK!

SKSHHHH

THAT ACTUALLY WORKED?!

I'M JUST GETTING STARTED.
BRMM-BRMMM!
K-CHUNG K-CHUNK

BRAWWNNN!

BLAHHHHRM

BA-BOOM!

CLUNK!

HA HA
BOOM!

CLANK!

HEY!

RETRAC
CLICK

CRAK! SNAP!

BOOOOOM

KILBURN SAID THEY WERE MEAN.
UNDERSTATEMENT OF THE CENTURY.

UH-OH.

BOFF!

PENG!

THE CROCODILLOS' TANK IS SOLID.

PUM!
PUM!

REALLY, REALLY SOLID.
DONK!
DONK!

LET'S FINISH HER.

WHAT IS THAT?

OH NO!

CLANG!

BOOM
BOOM

SKSHHHHH

THIS IS UNEXPECTED.
AND TERRIFYING!

BREAKING NEWS: DON'T HIT THE ANIMALS!
CRASH!
ON IT!

SPAK!

SPAK!

CRASH!

SKSSHHH!

CRASH!!

CRUNCH!!

SKSSSHHHH-
KRUNCH

CRUNCH!

THE CROCODILLOS AND ABOUT HALF THE FIELD CRASHED OUT.
THAT JUST LEAVES...

EVERYBODY ELSE.

NO PROBLEM.

KSSHHH

THIS SHOULD BE IT.

THIS **MIGHT** BE IT. THE TOPOGRAPHY IS UNNATURAL.
YOU BETTER DECIDE FAST!

HERE.
?!!!...&%!!
!!*!#$!!!

YES!
FOUND IT!
HUH?

WAIT.

WE DIDN'T WIN?

WE DIDN'T WIN.
NO, WE DIDN'T.

I TOLD YOU DRAY WAS SMART.
I CAN'T BELIEVE IT.

YOU GOT BEAT TODAY, BUT THERE'S STILL TWO DAYS OF RACE LEFT. SO SHAKE IT OFF, HETHERINGTON, AND LET'S FOCUS ON TOMORROW.

DID THE CROCODILLOS FINISH THE DAY?
NO, THEY CRASHED OUT.

BUT THEIR TANK IS STILL RUNNING. THEY'LL BE RACING TOMORROW.
OF COURSE.

ANOTHER DAY, ANOTHER SERIES OF NEAR-DEATH EXPERIENCES.
WE'LL JUST TRY TO STAY OUT OF THEIR WAY.

LET'S TALK ABOUT A CERTAIN SIXTH-CENTURY BC DECORATIVE NECK RING.

HUH. THIS LOOKS REALLY FAMILIAR.

IT'S THE PATTERNING. IT'S THE SAME AS THE PIECES WE EXCAVATED ON DR. HETHERINGTON'S PUCOON DIG. DO YOU REMEMBER THAT?
OH, OF COURSE!

HOW OLD WERE YOU THEN? FIVE? SIX?
FIVE.

AND YOU WERE A NEWBORN!
THAT'S RIGHT, DAD HAD JUST MADE ME.

PUCOON'S HOTTEST SUMMER IN A CENTURY. A HUNDRED DEGREES IN THE SHADE. EXCEPT THAT THERE WASN'T ANY SHADE.

YOU KEPT TRYING TO STAND IN PEOPLE'S SHADOWS, DO YOU REMEMBER THAT? YOU GOT CRANKY WHEN THEY MOVED.
I **DO** REMEMBER THAT!

AND YOU FOLLOWED ME AROUND **EVERYWHERE.**
ALL THE OTHERS SAID I WAS TOO LITTLE TO DIG! YOU WERE THE ONLY ONE WHO WOULD LET ME HELP. YOU TAUGHT ME HOW TO DOCUMENT SOIL ON THE MUNSELL COLOR CHART.

I COULD ALREADY SEE HOW TALENTED YOU WERE. YOUR PARENTS CAUGHT ON, OF COURSE, BUT I WAS THE FIRST TO SEE IT.

THEY WERE GOOD TIMES. DIGGING WITH YOU AND MY MOM. AND DAD ALWAYS NEARBY BUILDING STRANGE AND WONDERFUL THINGS.
I GUESS NOTHING REALLY WORKS OUT ACCORDING TO PLAN, DOES IT? YOU NEVER END UP WHERE YOU SHOULD BE.

ARE YOU KIDDING? THIS IS **EXACTLY** WHERE YOU SHOULD BE.
IF YOU DRIVE AND DIG LIKE I KNOW YOU CAN, YOU'RE GOING TO WIN THE IRONWOOD RACE ON YOUR DEBUT!

SO, THIS NECK RING --
WAIT, KILBURN. WAIT.
I NEED A SECOND.

WE REALLY NEED TO WORK ON TOMORROW.
I KNOW. I JUST -- I'LL BE BACK IN A MINUTE.

YOU OKAY?

WE MESSED UP TODAY.
WE GOT SLOPPY. WE DIDN'T DO A FULL SURVEY, JUST JUMPED ON THE FIRST SITE THAT LOOKED LIKELY.

MOM WOULD NEVER HAVE MADE A MISTAKE LIKE THAT.
SHE WOULDN'T HAVE LIKED US MAKING IT, EITHER.

THAT'S TRUE. SHE WOULD HAVE YELLED AND YELLED ABOUT IT.
YELLED UNTIL FALJEN GOT UP OUT OF HIS SARCOPHAGUS AND TOLD HER TO QUIT IT.

HE'D BE ALL, "AW, MAN, I JUST DRIFTED OFF! SOME OF US NEED OUR THREE AND A HALF THOUSAND YEARS OF BEAUTY SLEEP!"
TAP TAP TAP TAP

"HOW ELSE DO YOU THINK I KEEP UP THIS AMAZING BURNISHED GLOW ON MY DESICCATED FACE?"

WE CAN'T GO BACK TO THE ORPHANAGE, DIG.
I KNOW.
THIS RACE. DIGGING AGAIN. EVERYTHING'S DIFFERENT NOW.

WE NEED TO WIN THE RACE. GET THE ARTIFACTS TO THE MUSEUM, GET PERTON TO PUT US ON A DIG.

RIGHT.

SO WHAT ARE WE DOING OUT HERE? LET'S GO SEE ABOUT A PUCOON NECK RING.

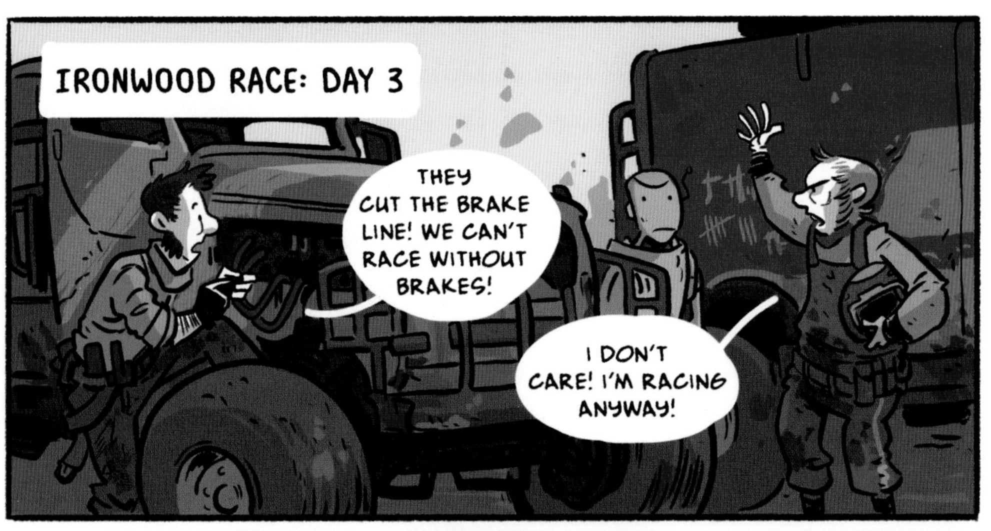
IRONWOOD RACE: DAY 3
THEY CUT THE BRAKE LINE! WE CAN'T RACE WITHOUT BRAKES!
I DON'T CARE! I'M RACING ANYWAY!

ALL RIGHT. WHO STOLE MY SPARK PLUGS?!

STATUETTE OF FALJEN
PUCOON NECK RING
AMASTROAN COINS
WINNER
TEAM HETHERINGTON
TEAM DRAY
TIME

I'VE UPLOADED THE LATEST MAPS. WE ALL SET?
YEP, ALL SET.

START. YOUR. ENGINES!
HERE WE GO AGAIN.

GRNNNNN!

BAM!

SPLUTCH

THUNK

TING
TING
TING

BOOM!

SKSHHHH!

CRASH!

YOU --
YOU OKAY?
UH.

SHUNK!

YOU'VE MADE YOUR POINT!

BLEEDING'S STOPPED.
GOOD.

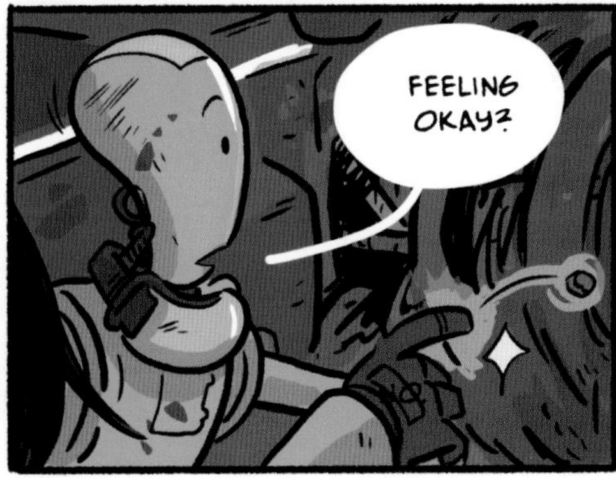
FEELING OKAY?

YEAH, I'M FINE.

SO. THAT WAS A CAR ACCIDENT.

IF YOU'RE GOING TO DO SOMETHING, DO IT PROPERLY, RIGHT?
WE'RE NOT HERE FOR A HAIRCUT.

WHAT ARE WE GOING TO DO? WE HAVE TO GET BACK IN THE RACE.

SITTING HERE'S NOT GOING TO GET IT DONE. COME ON.

SAFE TO SAY WE'VE LOST TODAY'S LEG. BUT IF WE CAN GET TO THE STARTING LINE BEFORE THE GUN TOMORROW, WE'RE STILL IN THE RUNNING.

THERE'S BOUND TO BE A TOWN NEARBY.

IF WE'RE LUCKY, THEY'LL HAVE A HALF-DECENT MECHANIC.

WE'LL JUST HAVE TO WALK TILL WE FIND THEM.

Marrickston
GATEWAY TO THE DESERT
POP: 430

HAMBURGERS
LET'S TRY IN HERE.

FR

THE COOK SAID FOUR DOWN FROM THE CORNER. THIS MUST BE IT.
REALLY?

OKAY, THEN.
SHRUG

KNOCK
KNOCK
KNOCK

HELLO?

IS THIS A MECHANIC'S SHOP?
YEP.
IS THERE A MECHANIC HERE?
YEP.

GREAT! WE BROKE DOWN A WAYS OUT OF TOWN. WE NEED A TOW AND A SERVICE.
CAN YOU PAY?
NOT EVEN A LITTLE BIT, I'M AFRAID.

NOT MANY PEOPLE CAN THESE DAYS. WORTH A TRY, THOUGH. JUST A SEC.

CHUNG
CHUNG
CHUNG

GET IN.
GUNG
GUNG
GUNG

WAIT. YOU'RE THE MECHANIC?
SINCE MY DAD SKIPPED TOWN, YEAH. I'M HEC.

I GUESS IT'S NOT SO DIFFERENT FROM ME BEING A RALLY-RACING ARCHAEOLOGIST.
IF YOU SAY SO.

SHUNK
SHUNK

YEAH, THAT. WE'RE COMPETING IN A RALLY RACE. THERE ARE A FEW... HAZARDS.

WHOA.

THIS IS A CUSTOM-BUILT SERIES SEVEN TANGO CHARLIE SIX-BLOCK ENGINE.
IT IS?

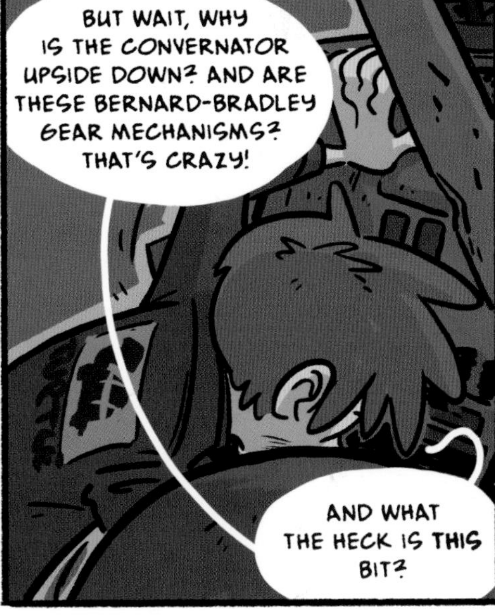

BUT WAIT, WHY IS THE CONVERNATOR UPSIDE DOWN? AND ARE THESE BERNARD-BRADLEY GEAR MECHANISMS? THAT'S CRAZY!
AND WHAT THE HECK IS THIS BIT?

MY DAD DESIGNED AND BUILT HER.
YOUR DAD IS A **GENIUS** MECHANIC.
YES, HE WAS.

CAN YOU FIX HER?
MAYBE. IT'LL TAKE TIME. I GUESS I'LL START WITH THE CAPISON COGS HERE AND FIGURE THE REST OUT AS I GO.

WAIT INSIDE. THERE'S A RECHARGING STATION YOU CAN USE.

SIGH.

CLANK
CLINK

BRMM
BRMM
BRMM
BRMM

THIS IS TAKING TOO LONG.
HEY, YOU'RE SUPPOSED TO BE SLEEPING.

WHAT IF HEC CAN'T FIX HER?
THEN WE DROP OUT OF THE RACE. NOTHING WE CAN DO ABOUT IT. CAN'T RACE WITHOUT THE BUCKET.

COULDN'T HAVE WRITTEN A USER MANUAL, COULD YOU, DAD?!
UGH! THIS IS TAKING TOO **LONG**!
FWUMP

WE SHOULD FIND ANOTHER MECHANIC -- ANOTHER TOWN.
THERE **ARE** NO OTHER MECHANICS, NO OTHER TOWNS.

YOU CAN SEE HER NOW.

WERE YOU ABLE TO SAVE HER, HEC?
SHE'LL BE FINE. SHE'S A FIGHTER.

I'M SORRY WE CAN'T PAY YOU.

IT'LL HAVE TO BE ANOTHER TIME.

WE NEED TO BOOK IT IF WE'RE GOING TO STAY IN THE RACE.

WE OWE YOU!
BIG-TIME!!!
THANK YOU!

IRONWOOD RACE: DAY 4

CAN'T YOU JUST WAIT?!
I'M SORRY, MR. KILBURN. BUT IF THEY'RE NOT HERE, I HAVE TO SCRATCH THEM.

BUT -- BUT -- OH, THIS IS A DISASTER.

ARCHAEOLOGI--
THEY'RE HERE!

THEY'RE HERE! THEY'RE HERE!
SHAKE
SHAKE

CUTTING IT FINE, AREN'T YOU, HETHERINGTON?

WHAT HAPPENED?! WHERE HAVE YOU BEEN?!
THE CROCODILLOS WON YESTERDAY, SO --
NO TIME, KILBURN. QUICKLY, WHAT ARE WE RACING FOR?

IT'S THE AMASTROAN COINS. HERE ARE THE MAPS AND SOME NOTES.
WHACK
GREAT, THANKS. WE'LL TAKE IT FROM HERE.

GOT A PLAN?
I DO. IT HAS THREE PARTS.

STAY OUT OF THE CROCODILLOS' WAY.
START. YOUR. ENGINES...

WIN THE RACE.

DRIVE OFF INTO THE SUNSET.
GET SET...

I CALL IT PLAN A.
THIS IS A PLAN I CAN GET BEHIND.

THEN IT'S UNANIMOUS. LET'S WIN THIS THING.
GO!

WHUD!
BRNN!
WHUD
WHUD!
GRAF
GRNNN

CHUNG
CHUNG
CHUNG
CHUNG

TWO FOR THE PRICE OF ONE.

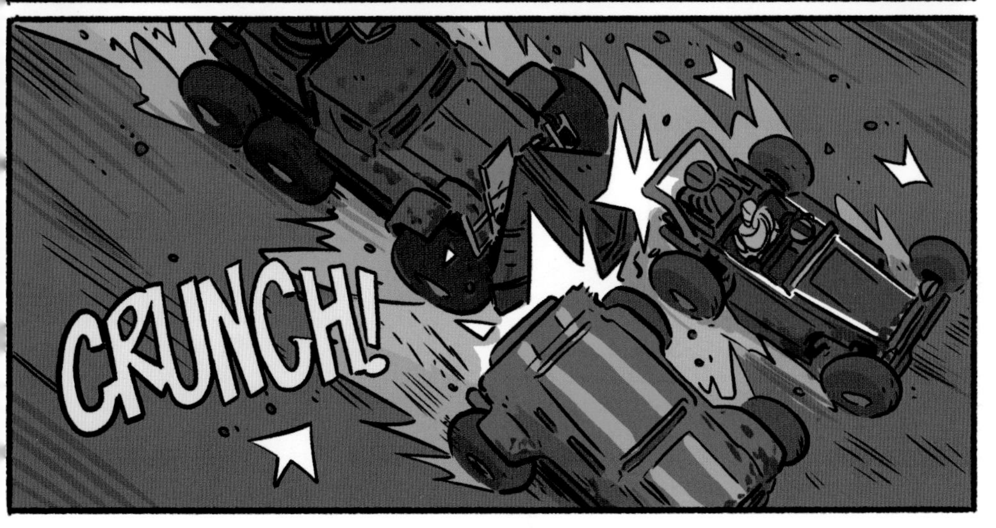
CRUNCH!

OH!
HANG ON, DIG!

CHUNT CHUNT
BOUB

HOLLIS! IF YOU'D BE SO KIND AS TO RETURN FIRE ON THE CROCODILLOS?
CHARGING. STAND BY.

CLUNK
HMMMM

CLICK

SPLORT

DANG!
EWWW.
BLOOSH!

I CAN'T MOVE.
HNNNNGH.

OH NO!

CRUNCH!

NO!
CAN YOU SEE, DIG? ARE THEY OKAY?

THEY'RE CLIMBING OUT OF THE WRECK.
THEY'RE OKAY.

SHARP LEFT!
ROGER.
GLOUP!
SKSSHH

SHARP RIGHT!

DO WE EVEN HAVE A PLAN B?

CHUP!
CHUP!
CHUP!
CHUP!

PING
PANG
PANG
PING
THEIR TANK IS TOO HEAVY -- THIS THING IS USELESS AGAINST THEM.

YOU'LL HAVE TO OUTRUN THESE JOKERS, CLEM!

GOT IT!
GRNNN!

WHUD!
K-CHUNK

CLUNG
CLUNK

THIS'LL THROW THEM.

BRNNNNN

CHNG CHNG CH
CHNG
OR NOT.

BOOM!
MANAGEMENT IS NOW ACCEPTING SUGGESTIONS FOR PLAN C!

WE'RE SO CLOSE.

CRUNCH
GAH!

HNNN --
WRENCH

SEE HOW YOU LIKE THAT!

YEP, THAT'LL DO IT!

CLEM!
LOOK OUT!

THUNT!

SKSHH

WHEW!
SKSHHHHHH

HOLD ON TO SOMETHING!

CHUNG
CHUNG
CHUNG

BOOM!

CLEM! MOVE!

BRN-BNNN
KSHHH!

CRASH!

CLEM...

YEAH, I SEE IT.

GRNNNN

EXTINGUISHERS?
READY.

BRNNNN

WHAT IS THIS PLACE? SOME KIND OF CAVE?
NO, NOT A CAVE.
IT'S A TOMB.
IS THAT IRONWOOD?
IT MUST BE.

SO WE KNOW WE'RE IN THE RIGHT PLACE.
UH-HUH.

HELP ME WITH THIS, DIG.

HE'S MISSING TWO FINGERS! I HEARD THEY WERE CUT OFF BY BLACK MARKETERS.

I DON'T SEE ANY COINS.
ME, EITHER.

I'LL LOOK OVER HERE. YOU TRY OVER THERE.
RIGHT.

HUH?

THIS IS AMASTROAN.

"FOR WHAT ELSE IS AN END BUT ANOTHER BEGINNING?"

CLICK

EERNNK

LOOK AT THAT, JUST LYING THERE.

DIDN'T HAVE TO DIG FOR THEM OR ANYTHING.
TROWL-LESS ARCHAEOLOGY? IT'LL NEVER CATCH ON.

LET'S GET TO THE FINISH LINE.

LEG WINNER AND
IRONWOOD RACE WINNER:
TEAM HETHERINGTON!

I'M SO GLAD YOU'RE ALL RIGHT, MS. DRAY.
IT'S JUST DRAY, HETHERINGTON. NICE WIN.

THANKS. YOU DID OKAY, TOO, WINNING THAT SECOND LEG.
I'M USED TO WINNING A LOT MORE THAN THAT. DON'T WORRY, I'LL GET YOU IN THE NEXT RACE.
LOOKING FORWARD TO IT.

I KNEW YOU WOULD WIN!

THE WAY YOU DRIVE? THE WAY YOU DIG? OF COURSE YOU WON!

QUITE A HAUL. PERTON'S GOING TO BE SO HAPPY ABOUT HAVING THESE IN THE MUSEUM.
YES. ABOUT THAT...

WE COULD DONATE THIS SMALL MOUNTAIN OF PRICELESS, IMPORTANT HISTORICAL ARTIFACTS TO THE MUSEUM FOR FLEETING RECOGNITION AND ZERO PROFIT.

OR! WE COULD SELL THEM TO A PRIVATE COLLECTOR AND MAKE A LOT OF MONEY!
SNAP

I'VE ALREADY GOT A CONTACT LINED UP. IT'S A SOLID DEAL. IT'LL PAY FOR OUR ENTRANCE FEE IN THE NEXT RACE. AND ALSO DISCHARGE MY CONSIDERABLE DEBT TO SOME MEN WHO WANT TO CUT OFF MY FINGERS.

YOU'RE IN DEBT TO BLACK MARKETERS? REAL SMART, KILBURN.
THE ARTIFACTS ARE GOING TO PERTON.

HE WON'T LET YOU DIG, YOU KNOW.
WHAT?

HE'LL SHAKE YOUR HAND FOR THE PHOTOS AND PUT YOUR NAME ON A LITTLE GOLD PLAQUE NEXT TO THE DISPLAY CASE.
HE MIGHT -- **MIGHT** -- LET YOU TAG ALONG ON A DIG. BUT HE'LL ONLY HAVE YOU CLEANING POTSHERDS OR MUNSELL CHARTING THE SOIL.

YOU KNOW HOW THE ESTABLISHMENT WORKS. PERTON WON'T KNOW WHAT TO DO WITH YOU!
EVEN IF YOU HAND OVER THE **LOST IRONWOOD ARTIFACTS**, HE'LL STILL THINK YOU'RE JUST A KID.

YOU'LL BE A FOOTNOTE IN HISTORY BOOKS ABOUT OTHER ARCHAEOLOGISTS -- PERTON, IRONWOOD, YOUR MOM.

BUT **WE** KNOW DIFFERENT. YOU'RE A RACE WINNER.

THIS IS HOW WE KEEP RACING.
YOU WIN.
YOU SELL THE ARTIFACTS.

YOU FINANCE THE NEXT RACE AND THE ONE AFTER THAT AND THE ONE AFTER THAT.
HOW ELSE DID YOU THINK AN ILLEGAL RACE WOULD WORK?
I KNOW YOU WANT THIS, CLEM. DIGGING, DRIVING. YOU BELONG HERE. THERE'S NO ROOM FOR THE MORAL HIGH GROUND.
YOU GET TO MAKE YOUR OWN RULES HERE. YOU DON'T HAVE TO LIVE BY YOUR MOM'S IDEAS OF RIGHT AND WRONG.

THEY'RE NOT JUST MOM'S.
THEY'RE MY IDEAS, TOO.

THE WORLD DOESN'T **CARE** ABOUT MORAL ABSOLUTES. THE GRAY AREAS WERE MADE FOR PEOPLE LIKE US.

I THOUGHT THAT IF I **SHOWED** YOU, YOU'D SEE IT THE WAY I DO. THAT WITH YOUR PARENTS OUT OF THE WAY, YOU'D SEE.
I THOUGHT THREE YEARS WOULD DO IT.

WAIT, WHAT?
KILBURN? WHAT DID YOU DO?

YOU **PLANNED** ALL THIS?

...

LOOK, THEY'D FOUND ME OUT. THEY CAUGHT ME STEALING ARTIFACTS TO SELL TO PRIVATE BUYERS. I TRIED TO CUT THEM IN ON IT, BUT YOU KNOW YOUR MOM.
I DIDN'T MEAN TO. IT WAS SO AWFUL. JUST SO **AWFUL**.
SHE WAS GOING TO TURN ME IN. I COULDN'T HAVE THAT.

THAT **WOMAN**.

OH MY GOD.
DID YOU --

HONESTLY, I DON'T KNOW HOW IT HAPPENED.

THAT'S WHY I COULDN'T ADOPT YOU.
THAT'S WHY I STAYED AWAY.

I WAS SO ASHAMED.

BUT THEN I DISCOVERED HOW TO MAKE IT RIGHT. THE REASON WHY IT HAPPENED AT ALL.

THE REST OF THE WORLD DOESN'T UNDERSTAND YOU. BUT I DO. WE'RE STILL A GREAT TEAM.
IF YOU WORK FOR ME, IN A YEAR WE COULD RUN THE PRIVATE MARKET.

KILBURN, NO. WE THOUGHT ALL YOU DID WAS ABANDON US.

BUT -- BUT YOU **BETRAYED** US.
YOU MURDERED OUR PARENTS! WE'RE DONE WITH YOU!
SIGH
I WAS AFRAID YOU'D SAY THAT.

SO I HAD MY MECHANICS ADD SOMETHING EXTRA TO DIGORY'S CENTRAL PROCESSOR.

I WANTED YOU TO DO IT ON YOUR OWN TERMS. BUT I GUESS WE'LL DO IT ON MINE.

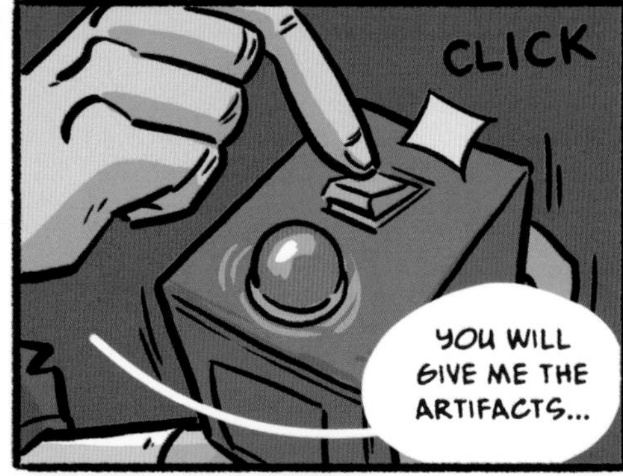
CLICK
YOU WILL GIVE ME THE ARTIFACTS...

OR DIGORY WILL DIE.

CLEM...

TAKE THEM.

I KNEW YOU'D COME AROUND! THIS IS --

THUD

RELAX, SMALL FRY. I'M NOT HERE FOR YOU.

AN HOUR AGO YOU TRIED TO KILL US.
THE RACE IS THE RACE. IT'S NOT PERSONAL.

I LIKE YOUR STYLE, KID. AND YOU STOPPED WHEN OUR TANK WAS ON FIRE, WHICH BUYS YOU SOMETHING.
NOT MUCH, BUT SOMETHING.
OKAY, THEN... WHAT DO YOU WANT?

KILBURN OWES OUR EMPLOYER SOME MONEY. WE'RE HERE TO COLLECT.

YOU'RE IN ON THE BLACK MARKET RACKET, TOO? FIGURES.
DON'T BE STUPID. WE ALL ARE. EVERYONE IN THE RACE.

OUR EMPLOYER WANTS WHAT HE'S OWED. GIVE US THE ARTIFACTS OR GIVE US KILBURN.
WHAT WOULD YOUR EMPLOYER DO WITH THE ARTIFACTS?
SELL THEM ON THE BLACK MARKET.

WHAT WOULD HE DO WITH KILBURN?
YOU DON'T WANNA KNOW.

HE KILLED MY PARENTS, YOU KNOW.
SO I HEARD.
HE DESERVES YOU.
SNAP

KNOCK
KNOCK
KNOCK

JUST A MINUTE --
CRASH!

YES? HELLO?

K-CLICK

GOOD GRACIOUS!

IT'S STRANGE TO BE BACK HERE. IT HASN'T EVEN BEEN A WEEK, BUT EVERYTHING LOOKS DIFFERENT.

YOU GOT WHAT YOU WANTED, RIGHT?
I DID. AND THEN SOME.
I'M AN ARCHAEOLOGIST AGAIN. I LEARNED WHAT HAPPENED TO MOM AND DAD...THE TRUTH ABOUT KILBURN.

BUT I DIDN'T THINK IT WOULD FEEL QUITE LIKE THIS.

MAYBE WE WERE BETTER OFF NOT KNOWING ABOUT KILBURN.
THAT'S A NICE LIE.

STILL, I'M NOT SURE I WAS RIGHT, HANDING HIM OVER TO THE CROCS.
THAT WAS KILBURN'S CHOICES COMING BACK TO BITE HIM.

I'M NOT SURE I'M RIGHT ABOUT KEEPING THE STAR OF THE EAST TO SELL ON THE BLACK MARKET, EITHER.
BUT TO BUY OUR ENTRY FOR THE NEXT RACE WE NEED TO --
I KNOW.

AND TO PAY A CERTAIN GENIUS MECHANIC TO REMOVE THIS --
TAP TAP
YES.

I WANT THAT MORE THAN ANYTHING. BUT I WONDER...
HOW WILL THIS CHOICE COME BACK TO BITE ME?

ORPHANAGE AND SCHOOL AND DEATH BY SLOW DEGREES...

OR MAJOR MORAL COMPROMISE AND THE MOST INCREDIBLE ADVENTURE IN RALLY-RACING ARCHAEOLOGY.
IT'S A TOUGH CHOICE.

YEAH.
BUT IT'S OUR CHOICE. NOT KILBURN'S, NOT PERTON'S, NOT MOM'S.

AND THAT'S ENOUGH.

For the diggers and the drivers.
J. B.

For Kazu, Kean, Tony, Dik, and the whole Flight crew.
D. H.

Library of Congress Control Number: 2016962982

ISBN 978-0-545-81445-4 (hardcover)
ISBN 978-0-545-81446-1 (paperback)

10 9 8 7 6 5 4 3 2 1 18 19 20 21 22

Printed in China 38
First edition, March 2018

Edited by Cassandra Pelham Fulton
Book design by Phil Falco
Color flatting by Julie Shanahan
Creative Director: David Saylor